EDITH OLIVIER

HORROR! HORROR! HORROR!

THREE TALES

THIS IS A SNUGGLY BOOK

Copyright © 2024 by Snuggly Books.
All rights reserved.

ISBN: 978-1-64525-152-1

"Dead Men's Bones" was first published in *Quakes: A Collection of Uneasy Tales* (1933); "The Caretaker's Story" was first published in *Monsters: A Collection of Uneasy Tales* (1934); "The Night Nurse's Story" was first published in *Panics: A Collection of Uneasy Tales* (1934). The stories have been ammended for the present volume.

Edith Olivier (1872–1948) was an English writer and an important social figure in Wiltshire, where she was born and lived her entire life. She published numerous books, but is most remembered for her novel *The Love Child* (1927). Other items in her bibliography include the novel *Dwarf's Blood* (1930) and her autobiography *Without Knowing MrWalkley* (1938).

CONTENTS

HORROR!
HORROR! HORROR!
HORROR!

THE CARETAKER'S STORY

THE CARETAKER did not finish his story, but his last lines were written more indelibly before my eyes than if they had been inscribed by pen and ink.

When I advertised for a caretaker for my seaside cottage, I was delighted to get a reply from my most level-headed and reliable friend, Jem West. Anyone he recommended would be satisfactory.

Jem wrote that Harter, who applied for my post, had been for several years the skipper of his cutter, and he only got rid of him when he got rid of the boat itself.

"Since then," the letter went on, "he has had two long voyages, both of which ended tragically in shipwreck. Once he was the only man saved. It hit him very hard, and he lost his nerve and wants to give up the sea. He'll suit you perfectly, for he's as honest as the day, and a handy man in every way."

When I saw Jem at the club a day or two later, I asked him whether he thought it wise to put a man who had lost his nerve into an absolutely empty house on a very lonely bit of coast. It would have been another thing if Horter had a wife, but, as it was, he would be day and night entirely alone in the house.

Jem didn't agree. He said that Horter's nerves were perfectly sound except for sea-going. That shipwreck had knocked him out because, it seemed, one of the crew had been his greatest friend, and Horter had got it into his head that he was in some way responsible for the man's death.

"He's got hold of some old seaman's superstition, and he's been reading *The Ancient Mariner* as well. He is a bit crazy on that one point, but otherwise he is a very steady old fellow, and I think a year or two on shore will put him right."

I interviewed Horter and liked the man, though he struck me as having lost his nerve rather badly. Not that he was at all jumpy. On the contrary, his manner was quiet and calm, but throughout our conversation no shadow of a smile crossed his face. He wore an expression of unchanging melancholy, and his sad eyes seemed to look through without seeing me. He was rather a remarkable-looking man with about him something of the decayed dandy. For instance, he wore an old shirt made of very fine and expensive silk, the sleeves of which had been cut off an inch or two above the elbow, allowing the frayed ends to hang loosely upon his arm. Instead of a belt, he had knotted an old Free Forester tie around his waist, and his spotlessly clean white duck trousers must have cost a lot when he bought them. Horter had delicate, refined features, though a receding chin gave a weak look to the lower part of his face. But for that, he would have been a handsome man. The deep-set eyes were of a clear blue, and the aquiline nose was finely cut. But it had a beak-like appearance from being inadequately supported by the chin beneath it, and in fact the man looked altogether rather like a sorrowful and haunted seagull. I almost expected him to spread his wings and sail quietly away into the sky.

He was touchingly keen to be engaged by me, but I could not feel altogether happy at the thought of this gloomy old bird sitting alone through the winter nights in my windswept cottage so near the sea. I warned him that it was a lonely place.

He shook his head.

"I don't mind being alone," he said. "It won't make me any lonelier."

He spoke thoughtfully, and his voice, which was always melancholy, did not change.

"Well, if you feel like that—" I began.

"I do," he said, interrupting me, but not rudely. He merely gave the impression that he was thinking aloud. I wondered about him, but I engaged him on the strength of Jem's recommendation.

The flat marshy bit of coast which lies between the New Forest and the sea was then far more desolate than it is today. My cottage was a tough little stone building which looked as if it had faced the sea for centuries, and had stood so long exposed to the wind and the waves that it had become an embodiment of the grey weather surging round it. It was a bit too bleak for me in the winter, but I spent all my summer weekends there, and I loved the place. It really was the only house from which I have literally been able to bathe out of my bedroom window. At high tide the waves actually washed my walls.

I thought to myself that if the sea had got on to Horter's nerves, he had by no means escaped from it now; but that, after all, was his affair.

Horter was not a good correspondent, though I generally heard from him about once a fortnight. He wrote an educated hand, which was singularly legible, but his letters were always short, and they told me little beyond the facts that he had received my fortnightly cheque and that all was going well at the cottage.

It was in February that he failed to write. I had been abroad, and my letters had not been forwarded, so that only when I returned home did I observe that Horter's acknowledgment of my last cheque was nearly a fortnight late. Another was almost due, and I sent that off a day or two early, with a letter asking how things were going on. There was no reply.

I felt anxious. Also I had a longing to see the cottage, for I had not been in Hampshire for nearly three months, and that year, the 26th of February, was so soft and spring-like that I could not resist the thought of my little house by the sea. I telegraphed to Horter that I should arrive in time for a simple luncheon of sausages and mash.

The cottage looked completely deserted. No smoke came from the chimneys. Doors and windows were rigidly closed and shuttered against the sunlit air, and the only sign of life was given by the great flocks of seagulls which drifted around and over the house. Their soft, harsh, mournful cries floated in the air like little drifting clouds transposed into sounds.

I walked briskly down the narrow shingled path, and tried the door. It was locked.

I felt nonplussed. Horter must have been out when my telegram came, and evidently the cottage contained neither fire nor food for me. Presumably he had gone away for the day, and I was at first annoyed with him for leaving the house thus unprotected. Then I realized that this was unreasonable. The man must go out sometimes, but as I walked round the cottage to the seafront I began to wonder whether Horter had indeed only gone out for the day. The shuttered windows were ominous, and I remembered those unanswered letters. Could my caretaker have deserted his post weeks ago?

The kitchen door faced the sea, and as I approached it, I saw something very disquieting. A little stream of dried-up blood issued from under the door. I sensed foul play, and went quickly to the window, to be faced by blank shutters. I could not see into the house.

My cottage was strongly built, as I have already remarked, and my shoulder failed to break in a door made to withstand the south-west gales. I walked round, vainly trying every possible place of entry. Even if my caretaker had left it, it seemed that my cottage was still eminently able to take care of itself. There appeared to be no way in. I looked at the thick short chimney, with a wild idea of climbing on to the roof and getting in that way.

As I stood there, thinking what to do, one of the seagulls which had been flying round the house broadened the circle of his flight, and swooped suddenly down upon me. With an ugly screech he went straight for my eyes. The brute! He meant to pick them out. I struck at him with my stick and broke his wing. He fluttered, and dropped into the sea, where he rocked to and fro, a few feet from the shore. In a moment half a dozen of his fellows were upon him. They looked threatening, and I thought they meant to peck him to death. I turned away, revolted, wishing that I had not caught him with my stick, although he had looked an extremely ugly customer as he made for my face.

It was an extraordinary thing to happen. Never in all my sea experience had I been attacked by a gull. I began to feel eerie and uneasy, almost frightened. Again my eye fell upon the blood which had oozed out from under the door. That decided me. I must get in.

I broke a window on the other side of the house, cutting my hand rather badly as I did so. More blood. I felt sick and tied my handkerchief round the wound. My luck was out that day. In spite of the gay sunshine outside, it was pitch dark in the hall, for all the shutters in the house were closed. I stumbled against one of the hall chairs, barking my shin. Furiously I unbarred the shutters and let in some light. Then I threw open the window too, for the house was utterly airless, and a revolting smell permeated it. Harter had certainly failed as caretaker. The sitting-room was dusty, dirty, and cold. I looked into it, opened its windows, and went to the kitchen. Just inside the door I caught my foot in something soft which lay upon the floor. It felt like a dilapidated feather bed, and I kicked the impediment aside and hastened to unshutter the window, for the stench was more than ever horrible. Then I turned and looked back into the room.

No wonder there was a smell. The place was crowded with dead birds. Eight or nine great seagulls lay piled up on one another in a state of complete decomposition. Their fallen feathers littered the floor. I stood there staring, aghast; and as I stared, I saw, pro-truding from beneath this heap of decaying corpses, a bone which was on another scale. It was a man's shinbone.

Feeling like some horrible ghoul I hurled the birds aside, and when I had done so, I had laid bare the skeleton of Harter. It lay upon the tattered fragments of his clothes.

A few hairs still clung to the skull, otherwise the bones had been picked completely bare. Feathers drifted over the face, disturbed by the wind which now blew from the open window into the room. The gusts disturbed too the pages of an old exercise book lying open upon the table. I had not observed it before, but the rustling roused my attention and I picked it up. I thought at first that the handwriting was quite unknown to me. It was very wild and untidy, the lines sprawling all ways. The pages were blotted with blood, and reminded me of those disgusting little bills which I had seen in butchers' shops, skewered on to joints of meat. I conquered my repulsion and forced myself to turn back a page or two. Earlier in the book, the writing was smaller, neater, and more legible. It also began to grow familiar, and when I reached the opening pages, I saw that they were in a hand which I had learnt to know during the past few months. Horter's careful script was unmistakable.

Then I forgot everything else, and I sat down at that kitchen table to read the story left behind by the caretaker.

"I have tried all ways to make atonement," the manuscript began, "and all ways seem blocked. They say that confession to a priest will ease the mind of any weighty matter, but priests don't often come my way, so here I leave this to any and all who after me shall enter this kitchen. I confess to them all. I keep no secret back. But when they read these words, who knows where I shall be? No ease of mind for me anywhere, but I swear that all you readers shall share this weight. It weighs too much for me, and it comes round and round, over and over again. There is no atonement, until I have told it all to some one. Yes, all. All. Everything. Did you know that I am Jonah born again?

No, I did not say 'a' Jonah, but Jonah himself, the very man. Down, down he went to the bottom of the sea, but I could not get there. Poor Allan went, and I scrambled on shore. We were together, he and I, both in the same boat. It was but a little one, like the city of Zoar, and I was Lot and got there safely. Lot's wife was a pillar of salt. Ah, the taste of it! I can never forget it. When I was alone on that island, I kept looking for him. I didn't forget him, and then, when he came, I didn't know him. How could I know him, for he had wings, and dear old Allan never was- an angel. Still I should have known him, if I could have gone on remembering him all the time. That's where I went wrong. I was hungry, and there were all those darned gulls about. They came so near that I thought they meant me to eat them. Manna from heaven, they seemed. Great white things coming down, and I couldn't help it. But oh! it was salt. Salt always in my mouth, in my belly, on my brain. A pillar of salt. That's me too. But I must get on with it. I've got to make it clear. You see I ate that gull because I'd stopped thinking of Allan, and when I had eaten it I knew what I had done. *The souls of dead sailors go to seagulls.* He flew so near because he wanted my help, and I ate him. Yes, I ate him. Now you know what I am——a cannibal. Can the priests cure that? That's why it all turned to salt—salt everlastingly. I can taste it now. It maddens me, and O Lord! this thirst! I can't stop drinking whisky, though that's salt too. Salter than the blood of seagulls, and I know the taste of that.

"A ship came and took me off, but they didn't guess I was a cannibal, or they wouldn't have had me on board. I said nothing, because I was afraid they would leave me behind again. But God knew. He knew me for old Jonah, and he wrecked that ship too. Jonah can't drown, and I couldn't go to the bottom that time either. Another ship lost and me washed up again. All my fault.

"But the gulls are around me here too. Dead sailors crying for their shipmate, and I have scrunched up his soul between my teeth. No wonder it tasted salt, but this whisky here is even salter. I hate it and I can't stop drinking it.

"There. I have confessed. That's all."

So far the writing had been unmistakably Horter's, but when I turned to the next page I saw that it had become wildly different, and now the page was streaked with mud and blood. There were fingermarks tinged with both.

"Those gulls are coming nearer and nearer. It's like that day on the island when they came all round me and I killed Allan's soul. Perhaps they're hungry too. I'll find 'em something to eat. But it's all too salt. They won't like it. It will make them thirsty, and then they'll go mad. Unless they like salt. Do you, gulls? Answer me, you devils. I believe you do. I can't make out what it is they are saying. Just calling and calling and coming round me with their huge wings, but they don't speak the King's English. It makes 'em very hard to understand.

"Now I've got them in the room. Ten or more. How they fill it, squawking round and round with their great wings like huge mill-wheels turning and turning. Shut the windows. Bar them. And I will confess to the gulls. Why can't they keep still and listen to what I say?

"Round and round and round and round, and the room too small to hold them. It's all wheels, and I shall be broken on them. They are coming so close and those wings are so wide. Wheels and wings. Wings and wheels. Flap, flap, out goes the candle, but it's not dark yet. The fire burns like hell tonight.

I believe they know I ate him and they are telling me to make atonement. Look, all you gulls. That's just what I'm doing. It's all in this book. My atonement. My confession. It's all down here. But what's the good of showing them that when they can't read it? Don't know the King's English. What language do they know? Words! Words! Words! Words mean nothing at all. Atonement is more than that. It's what you do, not what you say. And yet you can never begin to make atonement till the thing is done, and then it's too late. That's what it is with me. Too late. All turned to salt. I can't do anything more.

"They want food. So did I. Atonement. They want that soul I ate. Allan's soul, and they know where it is. They've come for it. I must give it back of my own accord. They shan't take it from me. It's salt blood they want. Life for life. Soul for soul. Food for food.

"Where's the knife? Hack it off. Hack it off. God. How it hurts! Now there's a gull gobbling it up. You liked that, didn't you? Now they're all coming at me. What a noise! What a crowd. And there's a crowd of knives too. Hack away, knives! There. I've got off another bit. It comes well off the thigh. I must get some more.

"These knives won't cut. So blunt. Now they are turning into beaks. Is that a beak or a knife? There's another, and another. Hundreds of them coming at me. Beaks without birds. They're clawing at me, biting me, tearing at me. It's Allan! When I ate him, I left the beak and I meet it again in the end. He's here. He's got me. Tearing, tearing, and, oh my God! it's hell! Torture! Allan! . . ."

The end was only blood.

DEAD MEN'S BONES

I KNEW that my grandmother was dying; and I, who had never seen death, sat fearfully by her bed wondering when the end would come. Would it be tonight? Could she live till tomorrow? I could not say. All I knew was that I had heard my parents say to each other that she could never recover, and that she must not be left alone. She had always been fond of me, and she wanted me to stay with her. And yet this silent watch filled me with restless terrors. I dared not move for fear of disturbing her, although I wished that she would rouse herself and say some word to break the silence of the room. The light tried her eyes and so we had no lamp, but the firelight shone fitfully, now flaming up and then dying down. As the flames came up they threw grotesque shadows on the wall. Granny was propped up against the pillows, and her face had grown terribly thin. Now and again its shadow was thrown, magnified and emaciated, on to the wall behind her bed. Her cap seemed all peaks, and her face was hawk-like. Those shadows fascinated me, but they frightened me also and filled the room with uneasy fears. It was a rough night too, and I had always felt frightened by the sound of wind howling round the house. It reminded me of something terrible which had once happened—something which I had remembered when I was surely too young to have had any memories of my own.

A memory of a previous existence? Perhaps.

Suddenly grandmother spoke:

"I don't like that wind," she said. "It reminds me of a terrible thing which once happened. Come and sit by me and listen. I don't want to die without telling someone about the most unforgettable experience of my life."

She lay silent.

"How old are you?" she asked.

"Sixteen," I said.

"I was only twelve, and Southover Church had not long been built. People used to come from far and near to see it, for it was unlike any other church in the countryside. Lord Southover had always been a great collector, bringing home treasures from every country in Europe, and when he built this Church for his native village he filled it with rare and curious things which seemed almost out of place in the little village. There were curious carved columns of porphyry which he had brought from a baroque palace in Spain; the twisted pillars of black marble had once stood in a Florentine church; and the deep dead colours of the mosaic pavement had shone on the floor of a house in ancient Rome. The font was roughly carved from a huge piece of red marble, and was said to have held libations in some strange heathen rite. The thirteenth-century glass in the windows had glowed like jewels in the walls of a chapel dedicated in a little Provençal town by a company of returning Crusaders. Grotesque episodes in the lives of the saints were carved in deep relief on the doors which he had found in a far-off town in Silesia. The church itself was like one of those baroque buildings that one finds in South Bavaria, and it was set among lines of quiet grey poplars, while close beside it a thicket of ancient yews suggested the site of an earlier burial ground.

"There had always been a tradition that an ancient church had stood among those yews; and, sure enough, as they dug the foundations, the builders came upon a large quantity of human bones. This seemed to prove that the new church was being placed on ground which had already been consecrated, and these bones were now carefully collected and placed in a stone sarcophagus or casket.

"A crypt had been built under the altar as a mausoleum for the Southover family. It had a low doorway leading into the churchyard, and over this was now placed the sarcophagus containing the ancient bones. As you came down the formal path which led to this door, walking between two stiff Victorian flower borders, you could read the elaborate inscription which told of the finding of these nameless bones, yet ended with the words:

"'And he said unto me, Son of Man, can these bones live? And I answered, Oh Lord God, Thou Knowest.'"

My grandmother stopped. I wished she would not go on, and yet I longed to know the end of her story. I sat breathless, and after a moment the thin old voice began again:

"My father," it went on, "was the first rector of the new church, and well I remember its dedication. That was a great day in our childish lives—a day of pealing bells, of robed bishops, and of public luncheons, for the whole neighbourhood came to see the church, which was already something of a legend. Southover never seemed to be a new church, and indeed it was not, for the outer walls alone had been newly built. Its interior was crowded with the creations of men of varying minds and differing faiths. It held the memories of a hundred generations. 'Far-fetched' was indeed the word to describe it, and many people called it out of place in the little English village; and yet it was its strangeness which gave it beauty and mystery. That was what Lord Southover had sought for and found.

"Yet I remember my own grandmother saying to my father (she was older then than I am now):

"'Such things should not be mixed. They don't meet well. They look wrong, and they bring evil. You cannot tell what you have let loose in your church.'

"My father laughed at her at the time, but sure enough, within two months of the consecration of the church, Lord Southover was dead, and his was the first coffin to be placed in the crypt under the altar. It was a long narrow chamber with, at the far end, a very grotesque representation of the Good Shepherd found in one of the Catacombs. A series of shallow recesses down the sides of the crypt awaited the coffins, and Lord Southover's was now placed in the innermost of these, in no way enclosed, but visible to anyone entering the crypt.

"Lady Southover was a beautiful creature, and to this day I can remember the impression made on me by the sight of her tragic beauty in the heavy mourning clothes which were worn in those days. She could not bear to leave her husband's coffin, and she insisted on spending hours in the crypt every day, kneeling beside it. Every morning, my father himself unlocked the crypt, and left the vault open for her to enter when she would. She always came and went by the private way which led from the Great House to the church, and no one saw her pass. Everyone kept out of the way. In the evening, my father locked the door for the night.

"Some little time had passed, when my parents had both to be away for a few days. I was always proud that, as the eldest of the family, I was already looked upon as able to shoulder a good deal of responsibility, and now I felt it fitting that it was to me, rather than to the old sexton, that my father committed the key of the vault.

"'Unlock the door at eight in the morning,' he said, 'and lock it at seven every night. Lady Southover won't come later than that, for it will be dark. Do not give the key to anyone else, and keep out of the way when Lady Southover comes.'

"Two days passed. I unlocked and locked the door with conscientious punctuality. Then came an evening when I went out fishing with my brother, and we stayed so long away that we returned to find ourselves in dire disgrace with our very severe old nurse. To bed at once, and without supper, was the sentence, and I was so mortified at being thus punished before 'the little ones,' that I forgot the crypt.

"I awoke in the middle of the night, and there swept over me the memory of that open door. The crypt had not been locked.

It was my fault. I don't think you can realise in these easy-going days, the overwhelming sense of guilt with which I then looked upon a failure to do my part in a family undertaking. For a few moments I was completely overcome with despair at the knowledge that I had failed in my trust. But as I grew more awake, I realised that it was not yet too late. I still could lock the door. The key was on my table, and the church nearby.

"I sprang out of bed, threw on a few clothes, and crept quietly downstairs into the garden. It was not dark. The moon was a few days after the full, and I never saw her shaped so uncannily. No beauty in her. She looked deformed and wicked. It was a windy sky, and the clouds fled one after another across the moon, so that her light came uncertainly, broken by patches of darkness. I went quickly along the garden path which led to the churchyard. The three old yews, their boughs spreading to the ground, stood like vast motionless presences, their shadows moving beneath them as the moon came out or disappeared behind a cloud. The words 'the shadow of death' came into my mind as I saw those dark terrible trees. The poplars behind them were, on the contrary, very thin and transparent. They were full of movement—little frightening breaths went through them, as though something invisible were passing.

As I ran up the walk to the crypt, a horrid swarm of bats rushed out, their twinkling flight making them seem like dark stars thrown up from some fretful little universe, to flutter purposeless beneath the majestic march of the distant heavens.

I ducked my head, covering it with my hands, and dived for the door of the crypt. As I put my hand upon it, I saw, for one second, in the darkness, a light. It was close beside the coffin. As I looked, it went. The darkness closed over it, and all was still. My heart too stood still. Terror seized me.

"Then I realised that Lady Southover might still be there. Perhaps it was earlier than I thought, for I had not looked at the clock before coming downstairs. It might be an hour when grown-up people were still about.

"Pulling myself together for a supreme effort, I held open the door, and called as loudly as I could:

"'Is anybody there?'

"The sound of my own voice completed my panic. The vault echoed with the words, the echo coming so close upon them that they were magnified and distorted. A chill silence followed them. But now I could wait no longer. I banged the door, locked it, and fled.

"For a few steps only.

"Then I realised that I had not given time for a reply. In my terror I had locked the door upon the living occupant of the tomb (if living occupant there were), and had left him or her alone for the night in that most gruesome place.

"I know that when I went back, I did the bravest thing of my life, but back I went.

"The pulses in my head were making such a noise that I doubted whether I could bear an answer from within. My own blood deafened me. But I was resolved that, when I called again, it should be with the door shut between me and that hideous black silence.

"I approached the door to find that the initiative was mine no more. From the vault, which a moment before had been so deadly still, there now issued a tumult which filled the churchyard. The door of the crypt was being violently shaken, and voices, many of them, were crying insistently from within. No: this was not Lady Southover.

"I thought the language was not really English, and yet I could make out some meaning in the hasty desperate words. The voices were unlike any that I had ever heard.

Were they shrill or deep? I could not say. They were toneless, and yet dominant as the wind, and they were urgent with an urgency I have never before or since imagined.

"'Open the door! Open the door! They have mixed the bones.'

"With the voices there came a thousand fluttering sounds, as if another host of bats were being driven against the door.

"I was shaking so much that, even had I wished to do so, I could not have put the key into the lock, but I knew that I could never, never open the door upon this unknown horror. I thought I was going to fall to the ground, and to save myself I clutched at the top of the low doorway. It seemed as if the whole church swayed with my weight.

"'Open the door! Open the door! His bones shall not rest with hers!'

"The agony in that voice was so terrible, so compelling was that cry, that in spite of my terror I found myself fumbling for the lock. The key touched it. Did I turn it? I do not think so, though I cannot say. But at the same moment the frenzied entreaty from within became a violent hurricane, and the door burst open with a crash. I was caught into the rush of a whirlwind, and the *Something* which came out of the crypt swept me helplessly along. Then the engraved stone at which I had clutched for support came thundering to the ground, bringing with it the sarcophagus behind. It felled me to the earth, and there I lay, helplessly pinned under it. The casket had broken, and the bones were littered all about.

"By this time the driving clouds had almost covered the moon, and it had become much darker. I lay under the fallen stone, my eyes staring into the uncertain twilight. I dared not close them, and I watched, rigid, unable to look away.

"But I could not clearly see the figures, two or three of them, which moved—

crouching, bending, turning over the bones. I was aware of their movements, but I could not distinguish themselves. They were so near me that I could feel a little stir of damp, cold air as they passed about, almost treading upon me as they went. I shrank away as far as I could from their wavering uncertain course, but I could not really move, pinned as I was beneath that stone. Perforce I watched their horrible gestures as they handled the bones one by one. Now they would lift one tenderly, fondling it with caresses which seemed indescribably evil; then they grabbed at another with ribald loathing and scorn, tossing it mockingly away, or hurling it brutally to the ground and trampling it underfoot. Sometimes they bent close to the earth near, dreadfully near, to where I lay; and then they whispered furtively, muttering and gibbering. I thought the scene would never end.

"Then the pain in my shoulder became unbearable. I fainted."

My grandmother was silent. I looked anxiously toward her. Was she dead or dying? Surely the telling of this story must have been beyond her failing strength. But no. She lay there quietly, her face less distressed than I had seen it sometimes during her illness, as though by speaking she had eased her memory of a heavy weight. After a few moments she spoke again:

"The sexton found me lying there next morning," she said, "and thought that I had been overtaken by the storm on my way to lock the door of the crypt. I never told my story to anyone, and it was always supposed that only the storm had loosened the sarcophagus."

"And the casket?" I asked. "Were the bones put back, and was it returned to its place?"

"It was not broken when they found it," replied my grandmother.

"Then do you think that the bones are there safely to this day?"

"I know they are not," she answered.

THE NIGHT NURSE'S STORY

N URSE WEBBER had tea alone in the Nurses' Sitting-room. The maid who let her in had told her that every nurse on the staff was out, and she guessed that it wouldn't be long before they had another call. "But they don't stop long," she had added cheerily. The patients keeps on dying, and the nurses keeps on coming in. It's nice to have plenty of change though, isn't it?" Nurse Webber agreed that it was, but when the maid had left her, she felt strange, sitting there alone after the friendly crowd in the Hospital. She suddenly felt that "private nursing" would be a cold and inhuman exchange for the stirring atmosphere of the great wards. She ate her bread and butter, and she wondered how soon Matron would have finished the "interview" which was occupying her, and whether there would be time before she appeared, to make a piece of toast on her knife by the fire. She thought not, and she was thankful that she had so decided when the door opened almost immediately, and Matron entered to find the new nurse "making herself at home" very demurely at the tea-table, instead of kneeling on the hearthrug scorching both her own face and a piece of bread.

Matron greeted Nurse Webber in her quick kind manner. She gave the impression that her friendly welcome was the prelude to some important piece of work which must be done at once. Nurse Webber felt that she had been plainly told that no time was ever wasted in the West Square Nursing Home. This did not perturb her. She had not forgotten her Hospital training.

"I am afraid I shall have to send you out tonight," Nurse, Matron said brightly. "I have no one else coming in till tomorrow night, and we have an urgent case. An old lady has had a fall and injured herself internally. Can you be ready by six? I must order a car to take you out, as there's no station anywhere near the place."

"I shan't take more than half an hour to unpack and repack," replied Nurse Webber: "and then I shall be ready to start as soon as you wish, Matron."

"I'll show you your room," said Matron, "and leave you to get on with it." And she wasted no more words, but left the new Nurse alone in the room with her trunk and her suitcase.

At six o'clock Nurse Webber was leaving the Home by the door through which she had entered it for the first time little more than an hour earlier. Matron came to see her off.

"Do you know Eustace Grange?" she asked the chauffeur.

"More or less," replied the man. "It's an out-of-the-way place, and I'm not sure of the road after Chisholme. But I can ask."

"If there's anyone out to ask on a night like this," said Matron.

"Well, we'll get there somehow. I've never been done yet, and I don't think I'm likely to be this time."

The dark wet November night had evidently had no effect on the spirits of the stout little chauffeur; and he gaily drove Nurse Webber away to her first private case.

They were certainly going to an "out-of-the-way" place, for they quickly left the main road and began climbing about the Moor, taking farm roads which zigzagged over steep hills, and turning ever into narrower lanes where no signposts marked the way. And Matron had been right. They met no one to ask.

Nurse Webber felt nervous. The journey was taking longer than she expected If the chauffeur, as he had said, did not know the way, by what instinct did he continue to turn and twist about this unknown piece of country?

She tapped on the glass.

"Do you think we are going right, driver?"

"I think so, Sister. It's somewhere out here, I know. We had to turn left in Chisholme, and keep on turning left and that's what we've been doing ever since.

"Let us stop and ask at the next house."

"Right you are, Sister, though there aren't many about, are there? I don't seem to think we shall find one till we get to the one we want. But I'll certainly ask if I get a chance.

And a chance came at the next corner.

A man was standing there, evidently on the look-out for a car, for as they approached he stepped into the road and signalled for them to stop.

"Is that the Nurse?" he called.

"That's right," said the chauffeur.

"I knew you'd never find the house, and I've been out here for more than an hour waiting for you."

"I'm glad you came," said Nurse Webber, in her sedate voice. "I was beginning to think we must have got off the road."

"I wonder you didn't," said their guide, as he got up beside the driver.

"How is the patient?" asked Nurse Webber, trying to assume what she thought must be the manner of an experienced private nurse.

"I fear my poor dear old aunt will hardly get through the night. In fact I don't know what we may find when we get in. I've been out nearly an hour and a half, and it's touch and go all the time."

They drove for another quarter of an hour, going downhill all the way. The road was damp and slimy, and the car skidded about most unpleasantly. Nurse Webber was immensely relieved when they came up against the bulk of a house, looming close upon them out of the darkness, which it made still darker. The car stopped with a last skid.

"Waynfleet is my name," said the man, as he opened the door for the nurse to get out.

The name seemed in some way familiar, but she could not remember where she had heard it.

"And my patient is Miss Parker, isn't she?"

"Near enough My poor aunt is not likely to answer to that or to any other name till the books are opened on the Day of Judgment," said Mr Waynfleet.

Nurse Webber's half-conscious dislike of him became definite. He spoke cynically, as if he were alluding to an absurd fairy story.

She said nothing, but went past him into the house.

The hall was elaborately and expensively furnished. Taste alone had been economized in its decoration The pile of the carpets was incredibly thick. It muffled all sound. Nurse Webber made her way through a crowd of gilt tables, Buol cabinets, velvet-covered armchairs, and marble pedestals on which stood statues of stout women carved by German artists. Every available space was filled by a crowd of *objets d'art*. The drawers of the big bureau were open, and a half-filled trunk stood beside it, while another, locked and corded, stood near the door.

No servant came to meet them.

"I should like to go to my room to change my things," said Nurse Webber; "and then I can go at once to the patient."

"I'll send a housemaid to you," said Mr Waynfleet; but without waiting to do so, he himself took the nurse upstairs and showed her her room.

"My aunt is next door," he said, "but they will come and show you round."

Nurse quickly changed into uniform, but the maid was at the door even before she was ready.

"I will show you where everything is," she said; and with the manner of one who wishes to curtail conversation, she swiftly led the way out of the room She showed Nurse Webber the kitchen, the bathroom, the lavatory, the housemaid's cupboard, and a small dressing-room in which a fire was burning.

"You'll have to heat up everything you want in here," she said. "We haven't any gas, so there's not a ring. Most nurses grumble about it."

"Have you had other nurses?" asked Nurse Webber. "I thought Miss Parker had only just had her accident."

"She's chronic," replied the other, in a tone of some irony. "One accident leads to another."

Nurse Webber disliked her too.

"May I go to my patient's room?" she asked.

"Surely, I'll put your supper in the dressing-room. What do you want for the night?"

Nurse Webber shortly ran through the list of her requirements—teapot and kettle, bread and butter, and a couple of eggs; she was shown the store of invalid foods; and she learnt where extra china was kept. It was a new experience to be alone in a strange house to shift for herself through the dark hours, and she felt rather helpless as she went at last into the sick-room.

Miss Parker seemed to be asleep. It was difficult to guess her age, for though the hand which lay upon the counterpane was not the hand of a young woman, yet her skin was singularly smooth, and there was no sign of grey in her thick black hair. Nurse Webber thought that the immovable face had that look of calm youth which she had seen on the faces of the dead, and yet Miss Parker did not in other ways look as if she were near death. Her face bore no signs of suffering or weakness.

The housemaid led the nurse across the room, and the two women stood side by side looking down upon Miss Parker's motionless figure. The invalid lay quite still, and seemed unconscious of their scrutiny.

Then the housemaid spoke, and her voice sounded curiously clear and thin. She bent over the apparently sleeping woman, saying, "Nurse is here, madam."

Miss Parker, who was lying on her back, turned her face to one side with surprising vigour. The gesture was pettish. It suggested dismissal, but she said nothing.

"Good evening, Miss Parker," said Nurse. "I hope you are feeling a little better."

"I don't want any of Mr Waynfleet's nurses," said Miss Parker. "You can tell him so."

"I hope you will let me try to make you a little more comfortable," said Nurse Webber, wishing that her patient would open her eyes.

"Between you, you will, in the end, I don't doubt. But not yet Not yet. I have still some fight left in me. I'm not so old and stupid as he says."

Nurse looked interrogatively towards the housemaid, to find the woman had silently left the room. The space where she had stood seemed now to possess an emptiness which was positive, not negative, as though she had left behind her the invisible mould of the form which had vanished

Nurse could get no further response from the figure in the bed, and she now busied herself with preparations for the night.

On a table by the window were some bottles of medicines and some charts She found that Miss Parker's temperature varied very little, and that it had been taken at six o'clock that evening. By whom, she wondered. It had then been a few points above normal. Apparently the patient was washed at nine o'clock each night, and then had a cup of ovalitine. Nurse Webber prepared the little meal, and she went to the bed. The invalid still ignored her, and the house was as silent as the grave. Nurse Webber felt very lonely.

Miss Parker made no protest while her face was sponged, but it was impossible to rouse her sufficiently to induce her to swallow any of the ovalitine; and Nurse Webber's first entry on the chart was the record of a failure to give the patient her usual meal.

As she turned from the chart, she saw that she had inadvertently dated the entry "*November* 6, 1932", instead of "1933." She wondered at finding she had made such a slip so late in the year, and then she observed that all the previous records showed the same error. Her predecessor had opened the page with the wrong date, and had so continued throughout. The persistence of such a mistake struck Nurse Webber as significant. There had then been no one in the house sufficiently interested to observe it.

In fact she began to feel that there was no one in the house at all. At any rate, all of its occupants must have gone early to bed, for though it was not yet ten o'clock, the only light which still burned seemed to be her own. When she carried the rejected cup of ovaltine to the sink, the light she turned on in the passage threw a faint sickly beam down the long narrow darkness, and as she watched its course she realized that if everyone had indeed gone to bed they had told her nothing of the geography of the house. What was behind the various closed doors? Where could she find anyone if her patient did indeed die in the night? Mr Waynfleet seemed to have thought this might happen, though she herself saw no signs of immediate collapse.

Nurse Webber went down the corridor, tapping one by one on each of the doors. There was no reply. The people in this house slept early and soundly.

She decided that there was nothing to do but to settle down too for the night, so she drew her chair close beside a shaded lamp which stood on a table some way from the bed, and she pulled out the patchwork quilt she was making. Obviously there was nothing to be done for the patient, and the long, lonely night stretched before her in a vista of uninterrupted needlework.

Now and again she crossed the room to look at Miss Parker, and to take her pulse. There was never any change, and the patient continued to appear quite unaware of her presence.

As she returned from one of these journeys, her eye chanced to fall upon the label on one of the medicine bottles. It was addressed to "*Miss Power*". Nurse Webber looked at it again. Surely "*Parker*" had been the name told her by Matron, and she knew it was the name she herself had used to Mr Waynfleet. She tried to recall his reply, and she seemed to remember that he had not quite accepted the name of Parker. What did it mean? It frightened her to think that she actually was not certain who was the patient she was watching in that horrible silent house.

And then she remembered the Letter of Recommendation she had brought from the Home, and which so far she had had no opportunity of presenting It was still in her case. She fetched it from her room, and read it under the lamp. It was clearly addressed to:

"Miss Parker, Eustace Grange, Chisholme."

Miss Parker. Miss Power. There could be no further question. The unresponsive figure lying in that bed was not the patient she had been sent to nurse, and, if not, the house to which Mr Waynfleet had led her could not be Eustace Grange? Where then was she now?

Waynfleet? Waynfleet? Yes, the name was certainly familiar. She began to feel as if she had always known it, and yet she could not say what associations it brought. Something sinister. Perhaps it was a detective story.

Feverishly she picked up her patchwork, and tried to concentrate on it.

When she next looked up, she saw a figure standing by the bed, gazing intently down upon the face of the sick woman. Mr Waynfleet had come so silently into the room that she had heard no sound, and he had crossed it without crossing her line of vision She certainly had not heard him open the door, but now as she glanced toward it she saw that he had not only opened it, but had shut it behind him. He ignored her presence, and after a moment he bent down to listen to his aunt's breathing. Nurse Webber watched him curiously. His back was towards her, and she could not see what it was that he was doing with something he held in his hand. The complete silence of his movements was uncanny. She felt as if she were watching a scene from outside a closed window.

And then, all of a sudden, she realized that he had quickly, and very deftly, thrown over his aunt's face a large white handker-chief, which he now drew tightly over it. There was a gurgling sound, and the fumes of chloroform filled the room. Nurse Webber sprang to her feet, and leapt across the room. She seized Mr Waynfleet's arm, and wrestled with him with all her force. She found herself thrown on to the bed, with the old woman under her, the smell of chloroform overpowering her too. But now her hands were on the handkerchief, and she tried with all her might to tear it from her patient's face. She would not see her murdered before her eyes. She fought wildly, and then Mr Waynfleet's hand closed round her throat. It seemed as cold as ice. She tried to bite it, but it eluded her, though it still gripped her throat like cold steel, and still the fumes of chloroform swayed about her like tipsy waves.

They vanquished her at last.

She opened her eyes, feeling broken and sick. The room was in utter darkness. Mr Waynfleet had evidently turned out the light as he went away, and he must have been gone for some time, for the fire, which had previously been burning brightly, had now burnt out. She tried to remember where she was, and what had been happening. As her memory returned, she realized that she must be in the room with a murdered woman. But had Miss Power actually been murdered? It might yet be possible to save her life. Nurse Webber crawled to the door and turned on the switch. There was no result. The light must be off at the main. Then her blood ran cold. She was petrified with terror. Still she knew she must do what she could. She was a nurse, and there lay her patient. Even in this darkness, she must get that handkerchief off. She began to feel her way round the room, groping for the bed. Her hand traversed a blank wall. Where was the bed? Where indeed was any of the furniture? Everything was gone. The bed, her chair, the table on which she had left her needlework, the sofa, the . . . The room was empty . . . empty. . . . All she could be sure of was that she herself had woken in darkness with a murdered woman somewhere nearby. And the murderer? How near was he? How soon would those cold hands grab her again? She was afraid to scream, for no one but Mr Waynfleet would hear her, and her cries would tell him that he had not killed her as yet.

Then she began to think that she could not still be in the room in which she had lost consciousness. Of course he hadn't removed the furniture, but had carried her out, and had thrown her into an empty room. Could she escape? She wondered if she dared try to get out of this silent room, to find herself face to face with the unknown terrors of the house outside. She stood very still, listening. A clock was ticking beside her. She recognized the sound. It had exasperated her earlier in the night as she had sat at work. But where could that clock be now, for the table on which it had stood had gone like everything else? It was that insistent little sound which decided her. She must get away at all costs, for surely it meant that Mr Waynfleet himself was nearby, with the clock ticking in his hand. Till now she had

moved slowly and cautiously, feeling carefully for indications of her whereabouts,
but now she almost ran round the room,
groping for the door. She expected to find
it locked, but it wasn't. Instead, it opened
so easily that she almost fell backwards as
it came towards her. Quickly she shut it
behind her, and was in the corridor. Here
it seemed rather less dark, for the outline
of the staircase window glimmered before
her as a guide. It showed her where the
stairs must be. She paused, listening. Again
she heard the clock still ticking a few feet
away. It had come out of the room too.
Frantic, she ran to the staircase, seized the
banister, and hurled herself somehow down
the stairs. As she passed the window, a cold
draught caught her face, and even in the
darkness she was able to see that one of the
panes was broken. How could this have happened, for certainly there had been no window broken when she arrived? As she fled

down the stairs, her mouth was suddenly full of dusty cobwebs. They clung to her face, sticky, and exuding a musty smell. She ran through them and reached the house-door. It was locked. She felt for the bolts and found them at once, but they were not drawn. It was not they which kept her prisoner. The door was locked on the outside. Then once more she heard the clock ticking at her side. This time she screamed, hurling herself wildly against the door. There was no response, and her shrieks went echoing up the stairs and added to panic. Then she clung to the handle of the door and waited.

Hours seemed to pass, and now there was indeed in the air, a faint promise of dawn. It was hardly twilight as yet, but it was possible to make out that the hall too was completely empty. The door and the staircase stood where they had stood last night, but everything else had vanished. All that rich ornate furniture was gone. As she wildly peered into the lessening darkness, Nurse Webber began to think that she must have come down by some other staircase, to find in the back part of the house, a hall exactly like the one by which she had entered.

Her straining eyes came to the staircase window, and she remembered that fresh stream of cold air which had entered by it. It could not be far from the ground.

"I'll break every pane rather than stay here another moment," she said to herself, and she staggered upstairs and felt for the bolt. She found it. It moved, and she flung the window open as far as it would go. Wisps of night mist blew into the house as she leapt on to the sill, and let herself down by her hands. It was quite a short drop, and she was free.

She stood up and listened. The clock had ceased to tick. She had left it behind her in the house.

She turned and tried to run, but it was heavy going, for the earth was damp and sodden, and dead wet weeds clung to her legs and bedraggled her skirt. The garden was full of last year's neglected growths. Several times she tripped and all but fell, but she found the gate at last, and got into the lane outside. Then she ran with all the speed she could summon from her quaking limbs.

A man was whistling, and she heard steps coming to meet her. There was an early morning sound of pots and pans.

Nurse Webber was face to face with the dairyman on his way to milk the cows. She threw herself upon him.

"Help me. Take me away," she gasped. "Where am I? Oh, get me away from that awful house."

She stood there in her nurse's uniform, her cap awry, and her teeth chattering.

"Why, Sister, what's happened?" said the man. "Where have you come from? How did you get here at this hour of day?"

"I had a case. I went there last night. That house at the end of the lane. Oh, it was awful. I can't go back there. Tell me how I can get away."

"At the end of the lane? What house?"

"The stone house behind the laurel hedge.

"What, Laurel Lodge? You can't mean that. That house is empty. Has been empty since this time last year when Mr Waynfleet murdered his poor old aunt and her nurse. But he swung for it . . ."

Then the dairyman saw that Nurse Webber had fainted in a heap at his feet.

A PARTIAL LIST OF SNUGGLY BOOKS